W9-AWR-681

RICHIE and the FRITZES

RICHIE and the FRITZES

by Marjorie Weinman Sharmat

illustrations by Marc Simont

HarperTrophy
A Division of HarperCollins*Publishers*

copyright

for Fritz who was once Duchess . . .
and for Betty, Blitz, Sad Eyes, August,
Dracula Dog, Clone, Leaps and Bounds,
Show Biz Dog, Porno Pup, and Rex

and of course, Dudley

RICHIE and the FRITZES

Chapter 1

Richie

May 3

Dear Journal,

I think Annie Alpert likes me. She probably thinks I'm the greatest! Because of my muscles, my A's, and my famous fish scrapbook. Annie likes everything about me including a few things she doesn't even know about yet.

Annie

May 3

Dear Diary,

I can't stand Richie Carr. I totally dislike him. More than bugs, more than itches, more than liver. Bugs don't brag, itches don't brag, liver doesn't brag. But Richie Carr brags all the time.

3

Richie

May 4

Dear Journal,

The way I can tell Annie likes me is because she pretends so hard that she doesn't.

Today I saw her walking to school. So I chased after her, kind of slowly of course. Then I yelled, "Annie!" She dropped a book. How about that? I ran to pick it up. "Hey, Annie," I said. "Let me do that."

"I can pick up my own book," she said.

"There's a special way to pick it up," I said. "Bend your knees and keep your back straight. I know these things. I'm an athlete."

"That's not all you are," Annie said.

DID YOU HEAR THAT, JOURNAL? Annie must have been checking up on me.

She must have found out I can play chess, spell *microgroove* without checking the dictionary, as well as high dive.

Annie Alpert likes me so much she can't stand it!

Annie

May 4

Dear Diary,

Well, I almost told Richie Carr off today. He made me drop a book and then he bragged when he tried to pick it up. How can anyone brag about picking up a book? Richie Carr can.

On my way home from school I told Frances what happened. "Isn't Richie Carr the worst braggart in the world?" I said.

"I think Richie Carr likes you," she said.

"Hmmpph!" I said.

Then when I got home, Mom told me that Fritz was lost. The back gate was open and he ran out after another dog and didn't come back.

I wish Richie Carr would get lost.

Come home, Fritz.

Richie

May 5

Dear Journal

Annie is down today. I mean *down*. She didn't even do her Annie Walk, where she hops every few steps or twirls in circles and laughs. I saw her in school, and she looked like somebody sad and droopy. Her dog ran away and Annie likes that dog almost as much as she likes me. That's a whole lot, Journal.

So I'm going to look for Annie's dog. Who else can Annie count on? And I'll *find* him. Because when Richie does something he does it right.

Annie

May 5

Dear Diary,

Maybe I'll never see Fritz again. Maybe some people took him into their house and they're moving to California and so Fritz is, too. If Fritz comes home I'll never make him take a bath again.

Richie

May 6

Dear Journal,

Tired! That's me. I've been looking and looking for Annie's dog. I mean I looked an hour and a half today for that creature. I, Richie Carr, have been to alleys, parks, stores, dumps, delicatessens, parking lots, and garbage cans.

Still, Annie said *thanks* to me today.

What happened was that I saw Annie in an alley. I said, "I'm looking for Fritz, too." And that's when Annie said, "Thanks!"

Annie

May 6

Dear Diary,

Mom and Dad put an ad in the newspaper about Fritz being lost. But I'm saving up my allowance so I can go to California and look for Fritz. Every day I think of something else I loved about him. Today it's his tail. I don't know why Richie Carr is looking for Fritz. How could someone like him be a dog-person?

Richie

May 7

Dear Journal,

I've increased my dog hunt. Three hours! I
added meat markets to my looking places,
and also under the benches of the school
cafeteria. I even drew a picture of Fritz,
because I draw very well. I put it up at
school under LOST.

Annie

May 7

Dear Diary,

It's been 3 days now, and I'm still looking for Fritz. Richie Carr is, too. He's strange, Richie is. I was at the supermarket asking if anyone had seen a black-and-white dog with a long tail and a sad face and there was Richie. "A very sad face," Richie said.
Oh, and Richie draws pretty good.

Richie

May 8

Dear Journal,

    No. 1: A sore knee.
    No. 2: A hole in my sneakers.
    No. 3: Sweat. Sweat. Sweat.

These are the things I've gotten so far looking for Fritz. The sneakers were guaranteed to last through 75 baseball games. I wish I had worn them out that way.

P.S. I think Fritz got married or something.

Annie

May 8

Dear Diary,

Richie has been walking a little funny. Should I tell him to look in his socks for a pebble?

Chapter 2

Richie

May 9

Dear Journal,

You won't believe what happened today.

Zitts came over in the morning and said, "Guess what I'm getting today."

I answered, "A skyscraper."

And Zitts said, "Wrong. A dog."

Then Zitts asked me to go to the animal shelter with him and his dad to help pick out a dog. Well, I've had enough of looking for a dog this week. So I almost said no. ALMOST. What if *Fritz* was at the dog shelter! I went with Zitts and his father. I've never seen so many dogs at one time in my life! I've never heard so many yelps and

15

barks and dog sounds. And I've never felt so sorry for so many dogs. All behind bars and wanting to get out.

"You can have any one you want, Zitts," his dad said. "Except for the big monsters."

Zitts kept looking at one dog, then another, then another. At last he said, "*That* one!"

That one was brown and white with a bushy tail. I didn't know what kind of dog it was. Zitts's dad went to get someone in charge.

Suddenly I saw something that made me stop. Stop like a red light, Journal.

Right there at that animal shelter I found Fritz!!!!

Black except where he was white, sad face, long tail.

I ran after one of the people in charge. Then I pointed to Fritz. "That dog belongs to my friend," I said. "He ran away a few days ago."

"No, he didn't," said the lady. "That dog has been here for almost a month." "Nuts," I said. But I kept staring at that dog. I was getting an idea! I could take him to Annie and hope she thought he was Fritz. After all, a dog is a dog. And Annie needed any Fritz she could get. It was perfect. This sad, droopy dog would get a new home. Annie would be happy again. She would have Fritz back.

Then I began to wonder. Do dogs have warts and moles and scars and stuff like people? Could Annie tell the difference between the dogs? Maybe Fritz had a pimple that I didn't know about. Still, he had been gone for a few days. Who knows what a dog can get and get rid of?

I wanted this dog, Journal. Now, how to take him home?

It was easier than you think.

Zitt's dad had to sign a paper and pay a few dollars for Zitt's dog. Zitt's dog in its previous life was named Brussel Sprouts. Zitts changed it to Wolf right then and there.) I said to Zitts's dad, "My mother and father want me to pick out a dog, too."

"No they don't," said Zitts's dad.

"Yes they do," I said. "They told me that if I found one I wanted, I could bring it home. And I found one."

"No they don't," said Zitts's dad again. He wasn't exactly listening.

"I love that black-and-white dog," I said.

"Love is what counts," said the animal shelter person.

I also had a dollar with me, and I told Zitts's father I'd pay him the rest next week. Then Zitts started with his *Please, please, Pops* routine that he's famous for in our neighborhood because it works.

Zitts's dad signed for two dogs;

I held my breath when Zitts saw my dog. Would he notice how much he looked like Fritz? But Zitts was too busy with Wolf.

My dog's name in his (yes, it was a *his*, I had forgotten to think about that) previous life was Duchess. Wild. How could a boy dog get the name of Duchess?

"What are you going to name your dog?" Zitts asked on the way home.

"Brussels Sprouts," I said. "Brussels

Sprouts? That's stupid?" Zitts yelled. "That's why I took my dog. I figured he must have had a stupid life with stupid people who would name him Brussels Sprouts. I want to give this dog a new life. Right, Wolf?"

Wolf and my dog were panting and drooling and moving around in the back seat. It was a crazy ride home. When we got to my house, I rushed out of the car and pulled my dog after me.

I started to walk to Annie's house. I had to give this dog-*return* him-to Annie right away. Before my mother and father knew I had him.

That walk to Annie's was the best walk ever. Because I, Richie Carr, was returning Fritz to Annie. Well, maybe it wasn't exactly Fritz, but it was close enough. All dogs have wet noses and fleas and they sniff and they wag their tails. Annie would think

it was Fritz and she'd be so happy she couldn't stand it.

But what if Annie just knew that this sad long thing following me down the street was in real life Duchess? Duchess of the dog pound. Poor Annie. Without a Fritz.

Duchess followed close behind me. He seemed to like me. He should. I was getting him a new home, and a lot of instant love.

I rang Annie's doorbell. Nobody answered. I rang five times. Duchess

23

barked. Uh-oh, I hoped his bark was like Fritz's. I hadn't thought about that.

I left a note at Annie's house. It was a super note. I knew she'd call me as soon as she read it. Then Duchess and I went home.

I tried to sneak Duchess up to my room.

"Who is that?" my mother asked.

Some question.

"I'm showing Duchess my room," I said.

"What if she makes?" my mother asked. My mother hadn't noticed that Duchess was a he.

"Duchess is a he and he's housebroken," I said. "The lady at the animal shelter told me he was. She also said Duchess was friendly, very good-natured, intelligent, obedient, and wonderful with children. She said the exact same thing about Zitts's dog. I think it's a commercial.)"

Well, you have to clean your room if she

messes it," my mother said. "Whom does she belong to?"

"He didn't tell me," I said.

The rest of the day I waited for Annie to call me. Duchess slept most of the time. At suppertime I left Duchess in my room and went downstairs. My mother didn't ask about him. I guess she thought he'd left.

"EEEEEK!"

That was my mother when she felt something warm and furry rubbing against her leg. It was Duchess. Then Duchess made this little puddle on the floor. Trouble, Journal. It went like this.

"Get rid of her at once!": my mother.

"Out! Out!": my father.

"I have to keep him a little longer," I said. "Just a little longer."

"Why?": my mother.

"Why?": Father.

"Because.": me.

I cleaned up the puddle.

Then I took Duchess for a long walk. He needed it. When we got home Duchess went up to my mother as if he liked her. This made a big hit, Journal. My mother bent down and patted Duchess and said, "Well, she is cute."

Duchess sat down and waited for lots of pats.

My father said, "Yes, she's a nice dog." I hadn't even thought about Duchess that

way. Cute, nice who cares? I only thought about the Duchess who was going to be Fritz. We all gave him a few pats because he expected them. Then my father said, "Time to take her home."

My father didn't know that Duchess was a he or that Duchess's home was our home. At least for the night. Because Annie hadn't called. I waited until my mother and father were watching TV and then I snuck Duchess upstairs to my room.

Well, I tried to keep that dog from barking. I tried to keep my rug dry. I tried to sleep with a wet nose near my face. There was more, but I can't write another word except to say that my father discovered Duchess at half past one in the morning and that belongs in my next day, Journal.

Chapter 3

Annie

May 9

Dear Diary,

Today I thought about Fritz's ears, both of them. They were always warm, and sometimes they quivered. Except for that, it was the same old Saturday stuff. Visited with Aunt Fan and Uncle Mack. Came home smelling of cigar smoke. Found a dumb note from Richie Carr.

It said, BIG IMPORTANT NEWS! CALL ME. He probably wants to show me a new fish picture. Ho hum. I'm going to bed.

Richie

Dear Journal,

My father isn't the kind of father who would send a dog away in the middle of the night. He's the kind of father who would take away my allowance for a week instead. I guess that's fair. Except my allowance was going to pay back Zitts's dad.

Anyway, my father said, "I am too tired to ask you why you have this dog in your

room, why it isn't home, where its home is, where you got it, and will it be gone by tomorrow morning." My father drooped out of the room.

Duchess climbed up on my bed. And we fell asleep.

In the morning Duchess and I went out. My mother and father said, "Goodby, Duchess," as if they felt that *goodby* was the key word.

I went straight to Annie's house. I rang her bell. Duchess was standing behind me. Annie answered the door. This was it!!!

"Guess who I found," I said.

Annie saw Duchess. She looked surprised. Then she squealed. She ran past me and hugged Duchess. Duchess yelped. Annie has a boa constrictor hug. "Oh, Fritz!" she cried. "You're back, you're back, you're back! I love you, I love you, I love you!"

Do you have to tell dogs things three

31

times? Annie patted Duchess and looked him all over. This was the test! Warts, moles, what would Annie find that Duchess had that Fritz didn't have? Or what did Fritz have that Duchess didn't have? Annie said, "He smells funny."

I hadn't thought of that. I said, "Well, who knows where he's been?" I felt on top of things, like I knew everything.

Then Annie asked, "Where did you find Fritz?"

I hadn't thought of that either. Dummo! I said, "It was tough. Tough. But anyone who can spell *microgroove* without checking

the dictionary can find a dog."

"But *where*, Richie?"

"There," I said, pointing backward. "Way over there."

"What was he doing?"

"Well, he was just sort of being a dog. You know."

I guess Annie knew. No more questions.

"Well, thanks a lot, Richie,?' she said.

I, Richie Carr, knew that *thanks a lot* means more than thanks a lot. I knew that Annie was thinking I'm the greatest. I knew that Annie wanted to kiss me.

But Duchess came over for pats.

When I left Annie's house, Duchess started to follow me. Annie had to run after him and grab him. I turned around. Annie was holding Duchess. And Duchess was squirming to get free. They both were sorry to see me go.

Annie

May 10

Dear Diary,

I got Fritz back! Richie Carr found him. Fritz smells funny, and we have to house-break him all over again. Do dogs forget things like that? I guess so.

I'm not sure Fritz loves me anymore.

Richie

May 11

Dear Journal,

Went to school. Saw Annie twice. She smiled at me both times.

35

Annie

May 11

Dear Diary,

Can't figure out Fritz. That smell won't go away, after two baths. He jumps up on furniture, and he chews socks. And I'm tired of cleaning up the puddles. Frances called it a "personality change. " I didn't know dogs had that.

Richie

May 12

Dear Journal,

Three smiles!!!

Annie

May 12

Dear Diary,

I just noticed that Fritz has one brown eye and one yellow eye. How come I never noticed that before?

Richie

May 13

Dear Journal,

Today was boring. My mother and father talked about Duchess. "A sweet thing," my mother said. I think they like him better now that he isn't here. So do I. Why is that? Maybe they miss him. Maybe I miss him.

Annie

May 13

Dear Diary,

Dumb is what I am.
That's why I never noticed that Fritz has
a funny bump on his leg that won't wash
out in his bath.

Richie

May 14

Dear Journal,

Saw Annie five times in school. Got five
smiles. Five out of five. Something big is
happening!

39

Annie

May 14

Dear Diary,

I've been thinking about Richie. I'm going to buy him a nice present for finding Fritz. Maybe a game or a book. Maybe a book about high divers. That would make Richie feel good because he is one. When I think of bugs and itches and liver, I will no longer think of Richie at the same time.

But I'd better ask him some more questions about finding Fritz. That might help me know why Fritz seems so strange. I don't suppose it will help me figure out why his tail seems shorter.

Chapter 4

Richie

May 15

Dear Journal,

Hooray! How do you spell that? Maybe it's hurrah. Who cares? Here it is in big letters.

ANNIE TOLD ME SHE BOUGHT ME A PRESENT AND SHE WANTS ME TO GO TO HER HOUSE TOMORROW TO GET IT.

This is really it. I hope Duchess will be at the door to meet me, because I MISS him in big letters, too.

Annie

May 15

Dear Diary,

The high diver book cost me two weeks' allowance. I bought a thank-you card, too. Fritz almost threw up over the present after I gave him his favorite dinner. I guess his favorite dinner isn't his favorite anymore.

Richie

May 16

Dear Journal,

I almost left a blank page for today. Blank is better than what happened to me. I got all dressed up to go to Annie's house to get my present. I wore my shark T-shirt. This was Richie Carr Day. A present for Richie Carr. Annie *liking* Richie Carr a lot. And no more chasing after Annie. Annie was chasing after Richie Carr, sort of. Buying me a present. Asking me over.

I thought about Annie and me all the way to her house. How much I wanted her to like me. How hard I tried. Like finding Fritz for her.

Then it hit me. Right in the stomach. On the way to Annie's house. I didn't find Fritz. All I did was play a trick on Annie, that's what I did. I was phony Richie Carr. Pretending Duchess was Fritz. And now I was getting a present for a dirty trick. I wanted to go back home. Maybe Annie liked Richie Carr, but I didn't. Even worse, poor little Duchess liked me. I must be a great phony, fooling a dog. (I read somewhere that it's hard to fool dogs.)

Well, my feet kept walking toward Annie's house. When I got there, my fingers rang the bell. Annie answered. My feet walked inside.

Duchess ran toward me and jumped all over me. Then he sat down and waited for his pats. Annie was looking at me like I was an A on her report card. Like I was the greatest. She had my present in her hand. Then she held it in front of my eyes. She could hardly wait to give it to me.

But now (and I'm gritting my teeth as I write this) I had to be the greatest. By

telling the truth, Journal, by telling the truth. Annie would hate me. But it was better than me hating me.

Duchess was sitting there watching us. Good. I needed a friend. I was getting up my courage. Annie looked so happy, so friendly, that I wanted to memorize that look forever, like the alphabet. She said, "Richie, I . . ."

She stopped. She was looking behind me. I looked behind me. The door was still open.

Coming up the walk, sniffing all the good old scents of home sweet home, was Fritz.

Chapter 5

Annie

May 16

Dear Diary,

Two Fritzes! Got to think. Richie ran off. Odd.

Richie

May 17

Dear Journal,

Shock is a bad thing. Even *I* don't deserve shock.

Yes, it was Fritz, the genuine real one-hundred-percent Fritz.

First thing, he sniffed Duchess. Seeing them together made my eyeballs shudder. Then Fritz slunk up to Annie and cried.

And cried.

I ran home. It wasn't a smart thing to do. But it felt very good.

I haven't mentioned today. I spent today trying to forget yesterday.

Annie

May 17

Dear Diary,

Number Two is my Fritz. I knew it right away. But I have to be very fair about this. Just because Number One Fritz was wrecking my house isn't why I decided against him. There's the smell, the bump, the eyes, the tail. The bark is a little off, too, when I think about it.

So who is he and where did Richie get him? And why did Richie run off? I wonder if stores take back books and thank-you cards.

Richie

May 18

Dear Journal,

I think I died today. I was in school. And Zitts comes up to me. And Annie comes up to me at the same time. Zitts asks, "How is Brussels Sprouts?"

Annie asks, "Who is Brussels Sprouts?"

"An ugly vegetable that shouldn't have been born, ha ha," I say. And I walk away.

Zitts and Annie keep on talking. Did I die on the spot?

Annie

May 18

Dear Diary,

Are you ready for weird? Here it is. Zitts told me that Richie got a dog from the animal shelter. He named it Brussels Sprouts. Zitts said that I'd be just crazy about Brussels Sprouts. I thought it was a vegetable joke when he said it. Now I'm not sure.

Here's some sad news. I was saving it until last.

My folks say I can't have two dogs. Number One Fritz has to go. But where?

Richie

May 19

Dear Journal,

I'm not dead yet, but I'm getting there. Soon. Zitts says his dad wants to talk to me. Something about honor and owing money. And Frances says Annie wants to talk to me. Something about Fritzes Numbers One and Two.

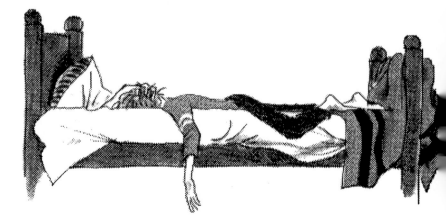

Annie

May 19

Dear Diary,

Decision. Tomorrow I'm going over to Richie's house with Fritz Number One and Fritz Number Two. There's something fishy going on. With Brussels Sprouts. With Richie running away. With two Fritzes. Tomorrow will be a big day.

Richie

May 20

Dear Journal,

What happened today? I finally died.

Annie

May 20

Dear Diary,

I hate Richie Carr. More than bugs, more than itches, more than liver.

Richie

May 21

Dear Journal,

What happened yesterday?
When Annie and Fritz and Duchess came over after school, Annie didn't even say hello. She looked like one of those characters in comic books who can turn into something else, some kind of monster. She looked like she was turning.

I invited her and the dogs inside.

Duchess came over and sat for pats. Annie asked, "Where did you find the dog you said was Fritz? Why did you run away when the real Fritz came home? Who is Brussels Sprouts? Do you have a big secret?"

Just then my mother peeked into the room. Duchess ran over for pats. My moth-

er said, "Nice Duchess. Good Duchess." Then my mother left.

Now Annie had a new question. "Duchess? Duchess?" It was all over.

"Duchess is Brussels Sprouts is Number One Fritz," I said. "I got him from the animal shelter. I got him because he looks like Fritz and I wanted to find Fritz for you."

Now Annie was out of questions. And into statements. "Richie Carr, you're rotten," she said. And she picked up Fritz and left.

Duchess came over to me for more pats. Well, somebody likes me.

Annie

May 21

Dear Diary,

I'm still too mad to write anything.

Chapter 6

Richie

May 22

Dear Journal,

I want to write something good right away so I'll tell you that I paid Zitts's father the minute I got my allowance. Also, I told Zitts everything. Then I told my mother and father everything. I think they're getting a lecture ready for me. But I don't care because they're letting me keep Duchess. I have plenty of cleaning up to do, but I'm getting busy training him. I take him for long hikes. I love him. He loves me, too. I don't even have to *try* to impress him.

Annie

May 22

Dear Diary,

I keep thinking about the dirty trick Richie played on me.

Richie

May 23

Dear Journal,

Duchess is the best dog in the world and sometimes I think I'm lucky, but not very. I won't mention Annie because I don't want to.

Annie

May 23

Dear Diary,

A perfect day because I didn't see Richie Carr. I guess he's busy with his new dog Duchess.

Richie

May 24

Dear Journal,

No puddles today.

Annie

May 24

Dear Diary,

Today I saw Richie Carr playing with Duchess. Duchess rolled over for stomach rubs and Richie gave him at least nine. You'd almost think that Richie was some kind of good person if you didn't know better.

Richie

May 25

Dear Journal,

Still no puddles.

Annie

May 25

Dear Diary,

Guess who I saw again. He was walking along, kicking pebbles, talking to Duchess, not showing off. I must be crazy but I almost liked him when I looked at him. Maybe Richie is a dog person just like me. Maybe the next time I see him, or the time after that, I'll speak to him.

Richie

May 26

Dear Journal,

Annie spoke to me! She said, "Hello." And we walked together down an alley. I told her I was training Duchess and that Duchess already knows what sit means. Annie patted Duchess and I patted Fritz.

Well, it's a start. Richie Carr may rise again.

Annie

May 26

Dear Diary,

I'm sure, I'm positive, that there are worse people in the world than Richie Carr.

Today we went for a walk. It was nice. Maybe someday I'll look at the fish scrapbook he keeps talking about.

Richie

May 27

Dear Journal,

Annie came over today. I only had to ask once. She looked at every fish in my scrapbook. She went wild over my piranha. Then we raced around the block twice with Fritz and Duchess. Annie said to me, "Richie, you're a dog person!"

I, Richie Carr, am a dog person? Annie Alpert *really* likes me, Journal.

And I haven't even told her yet that I can multiply 3,000 by 464 in my head and get the right answer!